Professor, Molebody's Potato Panic

Level 9 – Gold

Helpful Hints for Reading at Home

The graphemes (written letters) and phonemes (units of sound) used throughout this series are aligned with Letters and Sounds. This offers a consistent approach to learning whether reading at home or in the classroom.

HERE ARE SOME COMMON WORDS THAT YOUR CHILD MIGHT FIND TRICKY:

water	where	would	know	thought	through	couldn't
laughed	eyes	once	we're	school	can't	our

TOP TIPS FOR HELPING YOUR CHILD TO READ:

- Encourage your child to read aloud as well as silently to themselves.
- Allow your child time to absorb the text and make comments.
- Ask simple questions about the text to assess understanding.
- Encourage your child to clarify the meaning of new vocabulary.

This book focuses on developing independence, fluency and comprehension. It is a gold level 9 book band.

Professor Molebody's Potato Panic

Written by
William Anthony

Illustrated by
Amy Li

Chapter One

Professor Molebody's Potato Panic

"Come on, you're nearly there!" shouted Lily. "One on the right! Quick, on the le—" 'GAME OVER' appeared on the screen. Asha's jaw dropped, but getting the second-highest score wasn't bad. The crowd walked off to watch other games while Asha tried again.

Most days weren't complete for any kid without a visit to the Odd Box Arcade. It was packed with everything a kid could ever want. There were hundreds of video games, loads of junk food and the best fizzy drinks you could ever think of. The best part was that it was an adult-free zone.

Everyone had their favourite video game and Ellie was no different. She started each day by putting a coin into the old, rickety video game in the farthest corner of the arcade – Professor Molebody's Potato Panic. This game was nothing like the others. It was slow and out of date.

The player controlled Professor Molebody and moved him up and down in the soil, avoiding any potatoes coming his way. If he headbutted a potato, it was game over.

The top ten high scores were all Ellie's. She was a pro. She dodged potatoes like nobody else had ever dodged potatoes before.

Ellie had dodged 881 potatoes, almost her third-highest score, when Caretaker Rick shouted out that it was home time. He closed the shutters as the Sun went down and everyone went home for dinner.

As the Moon shone, a flash and a spark followed by a small little 'pop' came from the arcade. Something odd was happening in the Odd Box.

Chapter Two

The Glitch

The popping sounds turned into bigger bangs. It was coming from the electrical room. The flashes turned into bright light. The handle began to turn and the door started to open.

A slightly square block came through the gap. The slightly square block was attached to a slightly square body, and the slightly square body was attached to a slightly square face.

"Mr Blox, can you please hurry up? It's so cramped in here and more characters are still on their way," yelled a robotic voice. Mr Blox walked out, followed by one of the Space Intruders, Cowgirl Maxi, some Teeny Troopers and Globble. Globble went straight to the food stall and filled up. Nugget Nibbles were his favourite.

The Dirt Drifter Drivers and Larry Craft came out next, followed by Professor Molebody. Globble offered Professor Molebody some chips, but he'd seen too many potatoes during the day to want any.

"It feels so good to stretch my pixels outside of the game," said the Space Intruder.
"It feels even better not having someone controlling where I move!" said Mr Blox.

The characters gathered in the arcade to talk about their day in the games. The Dirt Drifter Drivers were rather unhappy with the number of car crashes they were in, the Space Intruder wasn't pleased with how many times he'd been zapped and Globble... Well, he hadn't been fed enough.

Professor Molebody had enjoyed his day. Ellie hadn't pushed him into a potato once. He went to grab a fizzy drink to celebrate.

As the Sun began to rise, the characters made their way back into the electrical room. One by one, they made their way into their video games. Caretaker Rick arrived and opened the shutters ready for a brand-new day.

Chapter Three

Trapped

"Caretaker Rick, can you help me?" asked Ellie. She'd arrived all fired up to beat her high score.

"What's wrong?" replied Rick.

"It's Potato Panic," she said. "Professor Molebody's gone."

"Hmm, that is rather strange. Maybe there was a glitch in the game!" said Rick. "I'll have to shut down the game for repairs."
"You can't do that! What will I play?" blubbered Ellie.
"Look around Ellie, there are so many games to enjoy!" said Rick.
"But they're not Potato Panic," muttered Ellie.
Rick wrapped up the game in yellow tape and unplugged it from the socket.

Ellie went to get a sad fizzy drink. She pressed Buckleberry Burst and stared at her shoes.

Sniff, sniff.

Ellie's ears pricked up. The noise came from behind the machine. She leaned across to see a pair of feet and a furry snout poking out from the back. She moved to get a closer look. The creature took a quick peep through its paws.

"Ellie?" it said.
"PROFESSOR MOLEBODY?!" Ellie screamed.
"SSHHH! You can't let anyone spot me! I'll be taken away!" insisted the Professor. "Please, you have to help me get out of here."

Ellie grabbed a swanky coat and a large hat and dressed Professor Molebody. Together, they made a dash for the door, waddled home and snuck up to Ellie's bedroom. Ellie hadn't had time to think, let alone ask the Professor any questions.

"How do you know my name? Are you even real? Where did you come from?" Ellie blurted out.

"Slow down!" said the Professor. "You play my game every day and I can see you through the screen – of course I know your name! And yes, I am real. That's a rather rude question."

"Where I came from is a difficult story to tell," explained the Professor. "There's a problem with the electrics in the Odd Box Arcade. It lets me travel through my game's wires into the electrical room, where I can enter the real world.

"When the other characters and I came out last night—"

"Other characters?" Ellie interrupted.

"Yes, other characters! When I came out last night, I didn't make it back into my game in time. I was getting a Buckleberry Burst from the fizzy drink machine. Anyway, the other characters can help me get back into my game tonight. Can you help me get back to the arcade?"

Chapter Four

Back in the Game

Ellie and Professor Molebody crept through the night to the arcade. Sure enough, the lights inside started to flicker and flash. The Professor knocked on the window. Globble's eyes and smile grew very wide – not because of Nugget Nibbles this time, but because he thought Professor Molebody had disappeared forever! He let the pair in through the back door.

"Hey, I know you!" said Globble with a mouth half full. "You're the girl that always plays the Professor's game! You should play my game – it's pretty much the same, except I eat the potatoes instead."

"That's a sweet offer, Globble, but I'm here to help Professor Molebody back into his game," chirped Ellie.

"Oh," muttered Globble. "You see, there might be a bit of a—"

"Problem," finished the Professor.

The Fixer

Fix the SUN

23

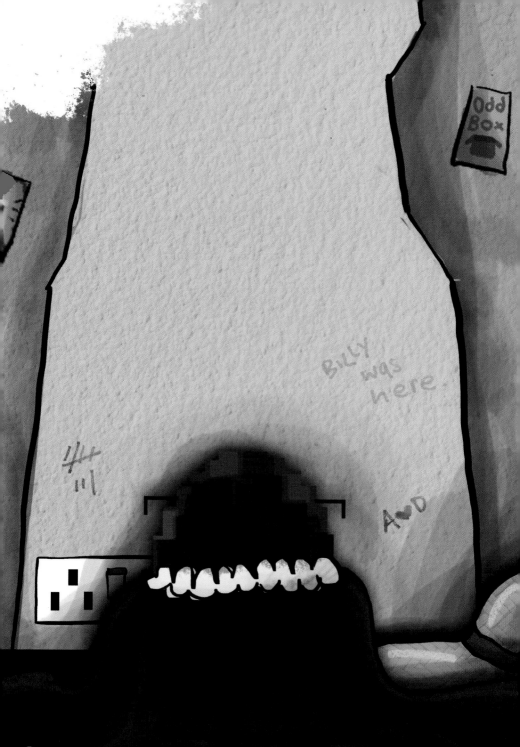

Professor Molebody was staring at an empty space in the corner. His shoulders slumped. "I'm sorry, Professor," said Globble. "They took your game away. They thought it was broken." Professor Molebody had no words to say. He had lost his home.

"Maybe you could stay in Globble's game? He said he had potatoes too?" wondered Ellie. "What if you stayed in Space Intruders? You'd be a great intruder; you know how to avoid being hit!"

Ellie kept trying, but the Professor was too upset. He dragged himself over to his swanky new coat and oversized hat, then plodded his way over to the empty gap. He covered himself up and went to sleep.

Ellie felt awful. If she had never told Caretaker Rick about Potato Panic, maybe Professor Molebody would have still had his home. She needed a plan, and she needed one before sunrise.

Ellie, Globble, the Teeny Troopers and Mr Blox planned through the night, until it hit Ellie. Why hadn't she thought of this before?

"Wake up, Professor, the Sun's nearly up!" whispered Ellie. "Keep your eyes closed, too – I have a surprise for you."
She led him out to a large field and told him to open his eyes.

"Where are we?" Professor Molebody asked.
"It's a potato farm," said Ellie. The
Professor's eyes grew wider and a smile
started to show on his snout. "During the day,
you can hide underground, and during the
night you can hide in... well..." Ellie pushed
open a bush. Behind the potato farm was the
Odd Box Arcade.

Professor Molebody had a new home – a real home. He hugged Ellie's leg before diving into the soil. He wiggled and kicked with his paws, as he made himself at home. He dug upwards to say goodbye to Ellie when he headbutted something hard. He looked up to see a potato balancing on his head.

"Game over, Professor," chuckled Ellie.

Professor Molebody's Potato Panic

1. What was Ellie's favourite game?

2. What did Globble offer Professor Molebody?

   (a) Carrots

   (b) Chips

   (c) Sweets

3. Why were the Dirt Drifters unhappy?

4. What did Professor Molebody get from the fizzy drink machine?

5. How do you think Professor Molebody felt when he couldn't get back into his machine? Have you ever felt like this? When?

©2021 **BookLife Publishing Ltd.**
King's Lynn, Norfolk PE30 4LS

ISBN 978-1-83927-400-8

All rights reserved. Printed in Malaysia.
A catalogue record for this book is available
from the British Library.

Professor Molebody's Potato Panic
Written by William Anthony
Illustrated by Amy Li

An Introduction to BookLife Readers...

Our Readers have been specifically created in line with the London Institute of Education's approach to book banding and are phonetically decodable and ordered to support each phase of Letters and Sounds.

Each book has been created to provide the best possible reading and learning experience. Our aim is to share our love of books with children, providing both emerging readers and prolific page-turners with beautiful books that are guaranteed to provoke interest and learning, regardless of ability.

BOOK BAND GRADED using the Institute of Education's approach to levelling.

PHONETICALLY DECODABLE supporting each phase of Letters and Sounds.

EXERCISES AND QUESTIONS to offer reinforcement and to ascertain comprehension.

BEAUTIFULLY ILLUSTRATED to inspire and provoke engagement, providing a variety of styles for the reader to enjoy whilst reading through the series.

AUTHOR INSIGHT:
WILLIAM ANTHONY

Despite his young age, William Anthony's involvement with children's education is quite extensive. He has written over 60 titles with BookLife Publishing so far, across a wide range of subjects. William graduated from Cardiff University with a 1st Class BA (Hons) in Journalism, Media and Culture, creating an app and a TV series, among other things, during his time there.

William Anthony has also produced work for the Prince's Trust, a charity created by HRH The Prince of Wales, that helps young people with their professional future. He has created animated videos for a children's education company that works closely with the charity.

This book focuses on developing independence, fluency and comprehension. It is a gold level 9 book band.

Additional images courtesy of Shutterstock.com.
Recurring images – be-bright (arcade floor), behind_green_eyes (arcade wall pattern), RaiDztor (arcade wall texture), vapadi (Ellie's top), sema srinouljan (Ellie's shorts), Offscreen (Professor Molebody's hat). P3 – Nik Merkulov, p6–7 – kasha_malasha, VL1, p8–9 – Skylines, wk1003mike, p10–11 – wk1003mike, p16–17 – wk1003mike, p18–19 – Dean Drobot, ping198, elysart, cluckva, wk1003mike, Kriengsuk Prasroetsung, p26–27 – Alex Leo, Alexander Mazurkevich, Praew stock, p28–29 – Praew, Nik Merkulov.